Copyright © 1999 by Nord-Süd Verlag AG, Gossau Zürich, Switzerland
First published in Switzerland under the title *Ein Haus für alle*
English translation copyright © 1999 by North-South Books Inc.

First published in the United States, Great Britain, Canada,
Australia, and New Zealand in 1999 by North-South Books,
an imprint of Nord-Süd Verlag AG, Gossau Zürich, Switzerland.

Distributed in the United States by North-South Books Inc., New York.

Library of Congress Cataloging-in-Publication Data is available.
A CIP catalogue record for this book is available from The British Library.

ISBN 0-7358-1156-3 (trade binding)
1 3 5 7 9 TB 10 8 6 4 2
ISBN 0-7358-1157-1 (library binding)
1 3 5 7 9 LB 10 8 6 4 2
Printed in Belgium

For more information about our books,
and the authors and artists who create them,
visit our web site: http://www.northsouth.com

Anne Liersch

A House
Is Not
a Home

ILLUSTRATED BY
Christa Unzner

TRANSLATED BY
J. Alison James

North-South Books

NEW YORK · LONDON

It was a beautiful autumn day. Fox warmed herself in the last rays of the sun. The hares scampered here and there. Wild Boar munched on acorns and chestnuts, and Deer nibbled on the last juicy grass in the glen. Only Hedgehog snuffled restlessly through the leaves.

"It will be winter soon," she said. "We have to keep that in mind, yes indeed, we have to keep that in mind. How do you propose we keep ourselves warm when the snow flies?"

"We could build ourselves a house," suggested Fox. "Then we could sit around the fire and play cards."

"We could eat roasted chestnuts," said Wild Boar, grunting excitedly.

"And every evening we could tell each other stories," said Deer dreamily.

"I could curl up in a warm corner and sleep all winter," said Hedgehog. "What a wonderful idea. We should start first thing in the morning, yes indeed, we should start first thing. There's no time to lose."

The next day the animals met in the glade and cheerfully set to work.

The hares gathered stones from the field. Hedgehog helped Wild Boar to get wood from the forest. Deer laid the stone to form a wall, and Fox mixed the concrete.

They worked hard, but they enjoyed it.

Then Badger showed up. "I see you are building a house," he said. "I can build excellent houses. May I help?"

"Yes, of course," the others replied.

The next morning when the other animals showed up at the site, Badger was already hard at work. "Don't just stand there, lazybones," he cried. "Get to work!"

So Deer and the hares ran off to find wood. But when they brought a pile to Badger, he wasn't happy: one log was too short, another too long, one too thick, another too thin.

Wild Boar collected stones. But when Badger saw them, he said they were all wrong too: one was too small, another too big. One was too pointed, another too round.

Disappointed, Wild Boar flopped down on the grass.

Badger went off to find stones himself.

Hedgehog whistled happily as she sawed a board.

"Stop that racket, you're out of tune!" shrieked Badger. "Besides, you are cutting the board crooked. Give me the saw. I'll do it myself."

Hedgehog headed sadly for a little clearing in the woods right across from the building site.

"Friends, it's time for a break," Fox cried cheerfully, and she brought a great pot filled with warm soup to the little clearing. Even Wild Boar came when he smelled the soup.

"I don't have time to sit around," said Badger grumpily, and he continued hammering and sawing.

The next day was no different.

"Good morning," the animals said to Badger.

"Sleepyheads!" he snapped. "Hurry up, would you, and bring me more wood!"

The hares headed slowly into the woods.

Deer and Wild Boar built a window frame. But Badger just shook his head. "It's not square," he complained, "and it's much too big."

So the two of them took their window frame and went over to the clearing in the woods.

The hares came back lugging wood from the forest.

"For heaven's sake, this wood is still wet!" shrieked Badger.

So the hares turned around and headed for the clearing, taking their wood with them.

Hedgehog and Fox arrived with paint and fabric.

"You must be out of your minds! It is much too early for curtains and paint!" raged Badger.

So Fox took the fabric away and headed for the clearing. Hedgehog rolled the can of paint along behind.

"Nothing is good enough for Badger," grumbled Hedgehog. "No, nothing suits him at all."

Completely discouraged, the animals sat and watched
Badger building the house all by himself.

"Friends," said Fox, "soon it will snow. We should at least
throw a roof over our little spot here."

All the animals looked at Fox. Now that was a good idea!

Full of enthusiasm, they set to work, laughing and singing all the while.

After a week, a small cottage stood in the little clearing. It was a bit crooked, and a few nails were bent. But that didn't bother anyone.

They sat happily around the warm fire, played cards, told stories, and ate roasted chestnuts. And Hedgehog settled in for her winter sleep.

Badger had finished his house too.
It stood right across the way from the
little cottage and looked really splendid.
Every beam was level, every nail
straight. In the evening, Badger sat at
the window, listening to the sounds of
happy laughter from the other animals.

Suddenly Badger felt lonely in his
beautiful house. For a long time he
considered what to do. Then, when the
first flakes of snow fell from the sky, he
had an idea. Busily he began to work.

A few days later, Badger knocked on the door of the little cottage. "Dear friends," he said nervously. "I have brought you a present."

"Look at that!" cried the littlest hare.

"Quite astonishing," murmured Fox.

"And it's all handmade," said Deer, impressed.

"It's a sled," explained Badger. "And there is a seat for each of you."

Mother Hare smiled kindly at Badger. "I hope you remembered to build a seat for yourself."

Badger nodded happily.

"What's all the uproar?" snorted Hedgehog. "For goodness' sake, Badger did that? What a nice surprise!" She snorted again, then went back to sleep until spring.

The other animals spent the winter sledding down snowy hills by day and sitting happily together by the fire in the evenings. And Badger, who kept the sled in tip-top shape, soon abandoned his own house and moved into the crooked little cottage with his friends.